Cherry on Top

Elise Noble

Published by Undercover Publishing Limited

Copyright © 2017 Elise Noble

v2

ISBN: 978-1-910954-56-0

Edited by Nikki Mentges, NAM Editorial

www.undercover-publishing.com

www.elise-noble.com

A balanced diet is having a cupcake in each hand.

CHAPTER 1

DAY FORTY-SIX of my new life. A gloriously sunny Friday. I had a cute-ish new flat, a new friend, and a new job with as many free cakes as I could eat. I should have been relishing my freedom, spending the evenings of my twenty-fifth year celebrating a narrow escape while drinking dubiously named cocktails.

So, why couldn't I forget the old Cherry Sanders?

Days one through five post-Craig, or "Crexit," as I'd taken to calling it, had been spent awkwardly avoiding my ex while I packed up my belongings from our shared house. By day six, having been forced to endure his side of yet another phone call with his new girlfriend, I was ready to snap. A puppy! They were getting a puppy together, and they'd only been shagging for two months.

Craig and I had been together since I was twenty-one, engaged for over a year, and when I suggested upgrading the microwave, he'd vetoed that because it was a "big step."

Day seven after Crexit found me living in a bed and breakfast with three suitcases, a family-sized box of Quality Street, and a migraine, and I'd been trying to put my life back together ever since.

"Still thinking about your ex?" Olivia, my boss, asked.

"How did you know?"

"Because you've just iced the word 'asshole' onto that cupcake."

I had? Dammit, I had.

"I'm so, so sorry. I didn't even realise."

"If it's any consolation, you've made a really neat job of it. Maybe we should start a new line? Divorce party cupcakes. You know, to help women celebrate their liberation with a touch of luxury."

"We could package them up with a bottle of champagne."

"And throw in a free voodoo doll."

A giggle burst from my lips, and Olivia soon put down her spatula and doubled up too. As she'd told me when I first began working for her at the Red Velvet bakery, I could either laugh or cry. Seeing as I'd had no luck finding a mascara that lived up to its waterproof claims, I'd switched to laughing while I baked and decorated. It was only when I got home in the evenings that I bawled my eyes out.

"I still can't believe Craig had an affair with his dentist. I mean, every time he was due for a check-up, he fretted over it for a week beforehand."

At least until Shelley Constantine took over the practice. Not only were her teeth fake, her personality and her boobs were too. And Craig suddenly developed a new fascination for dental hygiene and allegedly needed four fillings in eight weeks.

Even then it hadn't clicked. The cheating git still bought me flowers every Friday and talked about going on a mini-break to Rome for my birthday two months from now. If I hadn't suffered a PMT-induced craving for crispy wontons late one night and seen them snogging in his BMW outside the Chinese takeaway, I might have continued living in ignorant bliss.

"I'm not sure whether that's better or worse than catching my ex boinking his personal assistant on the dining room table," Olivia said.

"I'd probably have puked if I saw them doing the deed."

"I couldn't even move. She'd legged it out of his house before I managed to shout at him."

"I didn't shout at all. First, I was speechless, and then Craig insisted we should both be civil and treat each other with respect."

"Ah, the sensible approach. I was going to take that, but then Maddie and wine got involved, and we swapped out my ex's conditioner for hair remover and put boiled eggs in his curtain rails. He went bald and moved out because of the smell."

I'd met Olivia's best friend, Maddie, once or twice, and I could totally imagine her coming up with an idea like that.

"I'm not sure I'd be brave enough to pull that kind of stunt."

"It's amazing what you can do with the right motivation." The computer in the corner pinged, and Olivia rushed over to check the emails. "Yay! Another order. Four dozen cupcakes for an eighth birthday party. If they keep coming at this rate, I'll have to hire another assistant."

"That's wonderful. Who knew so many people would pay so much for cakes?"

"Not me, that's for sure. I always thought I'd have to start a bakery in London, but Nye's grandma and her friend Marlene convinced me that basing myself in

Northbury and offering mail order could work." She gave her head a little shake. "A hundred and twenty pounds plus delivery for forty-eight cakes. Crazy, huh?"

"That's my whole month's grocery budget."

"At least the cost of living's cheaper here than in the city."

"Don't you miss London?" I asked.

"The first time I tried living in a small village, I hated it, but Northbury's grown on me. The sense of community's stronger, and it's so much more peaceful. Besides, I still spend a couple of nights a week in London, so I get the best of both worlds."

My own move hadn't been quite so drastic. I'd grown up in the closest town, and when I moved out of home, I only got as far as Craig's house on the edge of the suburbs. Work had been a ten-minute drive away, at least until I got fired eighteen days post-Crexit. The posh hotel where I'd been a pastry chef had one of those display kitchens where guests could watch their food being prepared, and when I'd burst into tears for the third time, the manager called me through to his office.

"Cheryl, I appreciate you've had a tough time recently, but our friends here at the Henlow Hotel don't pay for theatrics."

Always friends, never guests, even though I'd overheard several of them laughing about what a pompous ass he was.

"I'm sorry. I promise I'll look happier in future."

"It's too late for that, I'm afraid. A guest complained, and as you're still in your probationary period, I've talked with Mr. Henlow and we've decided it's best if you move on."

Now, why didn't that surprise me? Craig's father had made it quite clear I'd only got an interview for the job because he went to school with the owner of the hotel, so it stood to reason they'd had a friendly chat about my future.

"I understand."

Relief settled in the manager's jowly cheeks. "I'll write you a good reference."

My biggest achievement in recent months was walking out of there without weeping. I saved that for the car and the checkout line at the corner shop where I stopped off to buy chocolate, ice cream, and a bottle of blackcurrant liqueur that happened to be on special offer.

"Bad day, love?" the lady behind the till asked.

In typical British fashion, I tried to downplay everything. "No, no, everything's—" Sniff. "Fine. I don't suppose I could borrow a tissue?"

The lady fished around under the till. "Here, keep the packet." She glanced back at the almost empty shop. "Do you want to talk about it? Sometimes it helps to get things off your chest."

"Not really. It's just that my boyfriend cheated on me with his dentist and they're getting a puppy together and then my boss fired me."

Her look said she regretted asking. "Ouch. That's a lot of bad luck. Have you tried burning your ex's clothes? That worked for my sister when her Barry moved in with the coach from his slimming class."

"No, we agreed to act honourably." Although clearly, nobody gave Craig's father that memo.

The lady leaned across and patted me on the hand. "Acting like a grown-up can be overrated, dear, but I'm sure you'll find a new boyfriend and a new job in no time."

"I doubt that. There's not much call for pastry chefs in Great Haseley."

"What about the bakery in Northbury? That's not so far away. Old Agnes finally retired, and a new girl's taking it over. She came in the other day and put a card on the noticeboard, looking for an assistant."

"Really?"

"It's right by the door. Here, borrow my pen to note the number down."

And that's how I ended up working for Olivia, even when I confessed all in my interview. She was remarkably understanding about Craig and didn't seem bothered by the way I'd lost my old job.

"Their loss is my gain," she'd said. "When can you start?"

Right away, and better still, Agnes's old flat on the top floor was empty. Olivia offered it to me rent-free as long as I opened up each morning. Living in Northbury had grown on me too—I was close enough to Great Haseley to visit my old friends but far enough to ease the ache in my chest just a little.

And did I mention the cakes?

Speaking of cakes, I still needed to ice another twenty for Ashley's hen party. I put the "asshole" mistake to one side and picked up my piping bag again, smiling at Olivia as I did so.

"I think I'm going to be happy here in Northbury too."

I had to think positive, right? Craig was firmly in the past, and this was my future.

CHAPTER 2

RED VELVET MIGHT have been a new business, but due to Olivia's connections, we'd had a steady stream of customers since we opened the doors three weeks ago.

"Thank goodness it's Saturday," Olivia said. "I know I always dreamed of owning a bakery, but I'm still exhausted."

"Me too. I'm going to sleep all day tomorrow. Perhaps Monday too."

The bakery opened from Tuesday to Saturday, eleven to five. Before that, we'd spend a couple of hours baking, and the courier arrived at four-thirty each day to deliver the goodies to our internet customers overnight. Eventually, we planned to put a few tables in the empty space at the front and serve drinks too, but for now, our efforts were going into perfecting the product range.

"I wish I could sleep all day, but I haven't got time," Olivia said.

"Big plans?"

"Maddie's organised a superhero day tomorrow at the hospital where she works. A whole bunch of people are dressing up as comic book characters to entertain the kids, and I offered to blow up balloons and help direct the volunteers to the right wards at the right time."

"That's kind."

"I want to bake a batch of cakes after we close to take too. Nothing fancy, just plain icing."

"Need a hand?"

"Are you sure?"

"It's not as if I'm planning to go out anywhere this evening."

"You're a lifesaver. I promised to help Maddie drop everything off at the hospital later as well." Olivia gave my shoulders a squeeze. "You'll forget Craig in no time, and then I'll treat us both to a night out. Deal?"

I managed a smile. "Deal."

I'd take her up on that in, say, a year or two.

"There, that's the last one finished."

I stood back, surveying our efforts. Ninety-six cupcakes, each with chocolate frosting and a dash of glitter. Hopefully, the patients and staff at the hospital would enjoy them.

Olivia held up her hand for a high five. "I'll just fetch the boxes to put them in."

She hurried off as my phone pinged on the work surface. Most people had ignored me post-Crexit, with only a couple of old friends checking in. Olivia said they were probably avoiding me because they didn't know what to say. Meanwhile, my inbox was full of discount coupons and adverts for things I couldn't afford, and my social calendar was empty. Last night, I'd lain awake watching the shopping channel, for goodness' sake.

But maybe things were looking up? Today's email

was from Sarah, my lab partner from A-level chemistry and now the physiotherapist to Great Haseley's men's rugby team. Her dream job, apparently.

"Thirty-nine fit men," she'd said. "And I get paid to put my hands all over them. Paid!"

"I feel like that about cakes, and at least I get to sample the goods."

For quality control purposes, you understand.

Sarah had grinned over her cup of coffee like the cat that got the cream, whipped with a cherry on top. "Oh, I get to sample the goods all right, and there's no danger of getting fat, either."

Once she'd handed me a napkin to wipe up the tea I'd spat everywhere, I regained my composure. "You're not serious?"

"Only the unmarried ones, obviously."

And now she'd sent me a message. Oh, please let it be an invite to the rugby club.

It wasn't.

FW: The Ex Files

Cherry,

I wasn't sure whether to send you this, but I thought you should know. I think Craig meant to send the email below to Russell, but he accidentally sent it to the entire rugby club mailing list. He's an asshole, babe, a huge asshole.

Sarah.

My fingers shook as I scrolled down, so, so tempted to

hit the delete button instead. The first thing I saw was a photo of me in my underwear, pink with red lace trim. My make-up was on, my hair curled, ready to go out for the evening. Craig had caught me by surprise with the camera, and he'd promised—*promised*—that he'd deleted those pictures.

And it got worse.

Name: Cheryl
  Rating: 3.5/10
  Snog/Shag/Avoid: Avoid.
  Reasons:
  - Okay in bed but takes too much effort to get her there.
  - Only likes fancy restaurants.
  - Obsessed with tidying all the time.
  - Spends ages tarting herself up to go out.
  - Clingy.
  - Always making cakes with rainbow sprinkles and glitter instead of proper food.

I scrolled down farther. Girl after girl. All of us rated with our flaws dissected underneath. That...that... I didn't even have words.

"What's wrong?" Olivia asked.

"My ex, my bloody bastard of an ex. He... He..."

"What? Cherry, what's he done?"

I waved my phone at her. "He seems to have started an email list with his mates where they discuss their exes. Only..." I screwed my eyes shut, hoping beyond hope that when I opened them, the picture of me would have disappeared, but no. It was still there, and worse, Craig had taken the shot slightly out of focus and it looked as if I had cellulite. "He's sent the whole thing to everyone at the rugby club. Everyone! And if Jonny Riggs got a copy, then everybody in Great Haseley knows, because he's the biggest gossip there is."

She leaned over my shoulder, and I cringed as I showed her the screen.

"So much for treating each other with respect. You know what this means?" Olivia asked.

"What?"

"The gloves are off. It's time for a little revenge."

The glint in her eyes made me nervous. "What do you mean?"

"He just insulted rainbow sprinkles and glitter. Nobody gets away with that. Grab that drum of corn syrup."

"What?"

"The big one. He lives in Great Haseley, right?"

"On the outskirts."

"And he's got a car?"

"A BMW, but—"

"Then let's pay him a visit. Your friend's right—he's an asshole. And soon he'll be an asshole with a professionally decorated vehicle."

I still wasn't sure about the whole idea, but Olivia didn't give me a chance to think before she bundled me into her car. She'd only passed her test a few weeks back, but thankfully she didn't drive fast.

"Do you think Craig'll be home tonight?" she asked.

"He always goes to the pub on Saturdays."

"Good. Left or right?"

"Uh, left. I'm not clingy, am I? I mean, I hated it when he left me on my own at parties, so I asked him to stick close, but he went out with his mates at least three times every week."

Russell, Daffyd, Raj, Steve, and Darren—the rest of the names on that email list. Daffyd had rated poor Sally Parker as two out of ten because she "wasn't great at sucking."

And that thought alone hardened my resolve. This wasn't only about me. It was about Sally and all the other girls they'd insulted as well. I directed Olivia into Craig's driveway, and there it was—his shiny new 5 Series, gleaming behind the hedge. We both hopped out, and Olivia opened the boot of the Honda.

"Corn syrup first?" she suggested. "It'll be nice and sticky."

"I'd say corn syrup on the roof, and then we can ice the bonnet."

Between the two of us, we managed to tip five gallons of syrup over Craig's pride and joy, and it ran down the sides and dripped onto the gravel. Olivia had even brought a spatula to spread it around a bit. Then we started on the rest of the ingredients. I iced "ASSHOLE" in foot-high letters on the front while Olivia drew a remarkably artistic dick on the back window. In pink. All of it in pink.

"Sprinkles next?" Olivia asked. "I brought the rainbow ones."

We stood back, laughing as we flung them all over the car. Respect and civility—what a load of bollocks. This was the proper way to do a break-up. The glitter came next, and I flicked it artfully over each window as well as the radiator grille.

"I brought chocolate icing too," Olivia said. "What do you think of piping it on the door handles?"

"Perfect. You do that, and I'll stick the mini marshmallows on."

Every adornment we added made my heart feel a little lighter. Turning Craig's BMW into a giant cupcake could never erase the way he'd violated my privacy with that photo, not to mention his hurtful words, but it sure did make the pain more bearable. Maybe I could send my own email out? A photo of the car, and a rating for Craig. One out of ten.

Snog/Shag/Avoid: Avoid.
Reasons:
- Lies about everything.
- Insists on chips with every meal.
- Ahem, performance problems.
- Doesn't understand the importance of rainbows and glitter and that sort of thing.

No, I couldn't go that far, but just thinking the words was cathartic. I stood back to take a picture or two for my own viewing pleasure. This would be a memory I'd treasure.

Sweet revenge. The day I finally stood up for myself. There and then, I vowed I'd never let another Craig into my life.

"Ready to go?" Olivia asked.

Just one finishing touch left—a row of cherries along the bottom of the windscreen. Something for him to remember me by.

"Perhaps we could do that night out next weekend?" Olivia suggested, grinning.

I reached out to wipe a glob of chocolate frosting off her cheek.

"I like that idea."

"Do you want a photo of you with the car?" Olivia asked.

"Why not? I could frame it for my wall."

"Or," a male voice said. "We could use it as evidence."

I backed up, and my eyes widened as I noticed the man in running shorts leaning against the wall behind Olivia. He raised one dark eyebrow.

"C-c-can I help?" I stuttered.

He folded his arms. "I was just wondering what the hell you're doing to my BMW?"

CHAPTER 3

"*YOUR* BMW?" I asked. "I don't think so. It belongs to my ex."

"Craig Altwood?"

"How did you know that?"

"Because I met him when the estate agent brought me round to view the house."

I took a step back and studied the car more carefully this time. Beneath the frosting decorating the windows, I realised the leather interior was a pale grey rather than the cream I'd picked out with Craig, and this car had a better stereo. Oh, hell. Now I felt sick, and not just because of all the frosting I'd sucked off my fingers.

"Oh my gosh. I'm so, so sorry."

Where did I even begin?

"We're both sorry," Olivia put in. "Her ex was a total prick."

The guy tilted his head to the side and grimaced at the bonnet. "I get that. But you can't just go around icing the guy's car."

She put her hands on her hips. "Craig sent a nearly naked picture of my friend to all of his mates, with a rating and notes on her performance. He's lucky we didn't rearrange the panels with a rolling pin."

"Except you got the wrong car."

"I'll admit there was a small flaw in our execution."

The guy sighed, then swiped one finger along the chocolate frosting and licked it off. Under the circumstances, that shouldn't have made my insides flip in quite the way it did.

"Look, as long as you help me clean up the mess, I won't take things any further, okay?"

Olivia groaned. "Can we come back tomorrow night?"

"That sticky shit'll run down into the door mechanism if you don't hose it off right now."

"But I'm supposed to be helping set up a fundraiser at the hospital. It's important."

He muttered something that sounded suspiciously like, "Why me?" then dragged a hand through his hair.

"Fine. You're excused." He turned to me. "I take it you'll be staying?"

"Yes," I squeaked.

After all, it was me who'd got us into this trouble. First by dating Craig, which was a huge mistake in itself, and then again when I didn't look closely enough at the car parked on the drive.

"I'll unlock the side gate. If you lived with Craig, I'm sure you know where the hose is." The man paused and turned as he headed for the house. "So, what rating did the prick give you?"

"None of your flipping business."

The door slammed as he disappeared inside, and I wished death were an option. Not only had I embarrassed myself in front of a complete stranger, but my boss as well.

"I'm so sorry," I said again once he'd gone.

Olivia burst out laughing. "The look on his face! I

know it's not funny, but...but...it is, isn't it? I mean, the car's like one of those cake wrecks."

She snapped a few photos on her phone, still giggling. Thank goodness she wasn't angry. I thought of my old boss back at the Henlow Hotel and couldn't help smiling myself. When a kitchen assistant accidentally put the wrong number of candles on a birthday cake, he'd gone an alarming shade of red—this little lot would have given him a coronary.

"A car wreck. I'd better grab the hose before the frosting hardens."

Olivia's face grew serious. "If it was any other day..."

"You go and help Maddie. I'll be fine, I promise."

"Call me every half hour, just in case this guy turns out to be a crazy axe murderer."

"You don't think...?"

She waved a hand. "No, no, I'm sure I'm just being paranoid. But seriously, call me, okay?"

Wonderful—I felt so much better now. Olivia waved as she pulled out of the driveway, and I almost ran after her and jumped into the back of her little blue Honda. Except the guy would probably call the estate agent, who'd call Craig, who'd gladly give him my full name, phone number, and date of birth. Then I'd have to explain my mistake to the police.

As promised, the side gate was unlocked, and I uncoiled the hose from its reel next to the back door. What a fabulous way to spend the evening—turning into a sweaty mess as I tried to rinse corn syrup off a stupidly posh car.

What the heck did they put in that stuff, anyway? From the way it stuck fast to the paintwork, I wasn't sure I wanted to eat it again.

"How's it going?"

His voice came from behind me, and I jumped so violently I squirted water all over myself. The final freaking indignity.

"It's not coming off very easily."

"Do you need car shampoo?"

Now he asked? "Yes, please."

He'd put on tracksuit bottoms and a hooded top now, and when he came back, he surprised me by squirting shampoo into a bucket and picking up a brush.

"You're helping?"

"It'll never get done otherwise, will it?"

"I'm not totally useless, you know, no matter what Craig said about me."

"Still stewing over that rating thing?"

"If it was horrid enough to make us drive over and, uh, frost your car, I'm hardly likely to forget it in a hurry."

"You came a long way?"

"From Northbury."

"Not so far, then. Been there long?"

"A few weeks. How long have you lived here?"

"Since last Tuesday."

"If I'd known Craig moved out..."

"He said he was moving in with—" He gave his head a quick shake. "Doesn't matter."

"It's okay, you can say it. He moved in with his new girlfriend. His dentist."

The stranger shuddered. "What kind of bloke thinks about sex while he's being tortured?"

"You're not keen on having your teeth looked at,

then?"

"I've tried everything—music, desensitisation, hypnosis, sedation. Nothing works."

"Nothing?" I couldn't help peering at his teeth, and for a man with a dental phobia, they looked remarkably white.

"I tend to use vodka now." He leaned over to pick at the windscreen. "What the hell did you make this icing with? Tar?"

"Icing sugar, butter, melted chocolate, and a drop of coffee."

"It was a rhetorical question. This shit had better come off—I need the car for work on Monday."

"What do you do?"

He flashed those teeth at me. "Modelling gig."

Well, it should have been obvious, really. The chiselled jaw, the piercing blue eyes, the way his jogging bottoms clung to his well-toned backside when he bent over to scrub the bonnet. Not that I'd been paying much attention. In fact, I'd barely glanced at it.

"You do that full-time?" I asked.

"At the moment. Pass me that sponge, would you? Are you going to tell me your rating yet?"

I plucked the dripping sponge from the bucket, and resisted the urge to hurl it at him. "Stop being nosey."

"Come on, you've got to give me a hint." He stooped over the front of the car. "Pink glitter? Was this dentist male or female?"

"Female. And the glitter was one of Craig's complaints. Apparently, I only make sparkly cakes rather than real food."

"I didn't even get any cake."

"I'll make you a cake, okay? As a sort of...I don't

know...apology."

"One of the downsides of my job—I have to watch my figure."

He said it in such a camp voice I couldn't help laughing.

"We've developed a range of low-fat pastries for the socialites in Northbury."

"We?"

"Olivia and me. She owns the bakery there."

Speaking of Olivia, my phone buzzed with a text from her checking I was still alive. I replied in the affirmative but carefully left out the bit about Car Guy's career.

"So you didn't go out and buy all this crap to tip over my car specially?" he asked.

"No, it was an impulse thing. Someone forwarded me Craig's disgusting email, and we both saw red. It wasn't just me on it, either. They've been trashing their exes for ages by the looks of things."

His voice softened a little. "I wish I hadn't agreed to buy his curtains now."

I glanced up, and sure enough, familiar patterns taunted me. Maroon-and-cream stripes at one window, abstract florals in another. "I picked those out. The fabric for the master bedroom came from Italy."

"Guess that's not so bad, then. If it's any consolation, I turned down his offer to sell the rest of the furniture. I think he put it into storage."

I'd paid for half of it, more if you counted the carpets, and Craig had never offered me a penny. Hearing he wasn't even using it while I lived with an Agnes-circa-nineteen-eighty-style three-piece suite only added insult to injury.

Darkness was creeping in by the time we restored the car to its former glory. I gave it one last swipe with a chamois and stepped back, exhausted.

"There, done." I covered my mouth as I yawned. "I'm never attempting the whole revenge thing again."

"You went about it all wrong, you know that?"

"Yes, I do realise." I counted off on my fingers. "Wrong car. Wrong owner. Not enough alcohol. But thanks for being so understanding about everything."

"I'm sorry you got screwed over."

"According to Craig, I wasn't very good at that, either." I clapped a hand over my mouth. "Can you just forget I said that part? I'd better call a cab."

"Do you want to wait inside?"

"I'm not sure that's a good idea."

"I'm not going to chop up your body and bury you under the patio, if that's what your friend was worried about earlier."

"There isn't a patio. It's decking."

He shook his head and smiled faintly. "Come on. It wouldn't be gentlemanly of me to leave you out here in the dark by yourself. I might even be able to help with the alcohol part."

Oh, what the heck. I didn't want to stand outside by myself either, mainly in case any of my old neighbours wandered past.

Or worse, somebody connected with the Great Haseley rugby team.

CHAPTER 4

"I DON'T EVEN know your name," I said to the guy as I followed him into my old living room, now empty save for a sectional sofa and a large television. Craig's framed picture of Lara Croft was gone, replaced by a three-foot-wide print of the universe, which I had to admit was more tasteful even if it didn't match the curtains.

The not-quite-stranger turned and held out a hand for me to shake. "Lachlan Manning."

As his hand engulfed mine, my legs went slightly wobbly and my heart began to beat faster. What was wrong with me? Was it normal to react to a man's touch like that? I never had with Craig, but Craig could never have been described as catwalk-ready. More pub-ready.

"Cheryl Sanders. Most people call me Cherry." It matched my hair colour, a deep red.

"Do I count as 'most people'?"

"I guess."

A small smile flickered at one corner of his lips. "What do you want to drink? Wine? Or are you ready for the hard stuff?"

At his words, my gaze dropped involuntarily to his crotch, and I forced it back up to his face. "Wine's good, thank you very much."

His smirk said he'd caught my little faux pas. "Red or white?"

"White, if you've got it. Just a small glass. I'd better call that cab."

"Yes, you better had."

Except my feet decided otherwise and followed him through to the kitchen. Okay, so I was curious to see whether the minimalist theme continued through there. Two chairs at the breakfast bar, a fruit bowl on the work surface containing two apples and a banana, a fancy-looking blender. That was it.

"You didn't bring a lot of stuff."

"I don't like clutter. Besides, my old flat was smaller, and I'm not used to having this much space."

But he had another space print on the wall opposite the sink, a spot where I'd once hung a framed cartoon of a redhead who may have looked a tiny bit like me saying to her boyfriend, "When I said I wanted you to treat me like a woman, I didn't mean buy me a new dishcloth." Craig never had taken the hint.

I pointed at Lachlan's replacement picture. "What planet is that?"

"It's not a planet. It's one of Jupiter's moons. Ganymede. The largest moon in our solar system, and the only one with a magnetic field."

"You like that kind of thing? The solar system, I mean."

"I find it fascinating. There's a whole universe out there, and we've barely scratched the surface. How was it created? What's it made of? How does it work? And perhaps most curious—are we alone?"

"Do you think we are?"

He slid a drink over to me before he answered.

"I think it would be arrogant to even suggest that. There are trillions of planets just in our galaxy, and over two hundred billion galaxies that we know of. How can we possibly be the only one with intelligent life?"

Intelligent life? He couldn't have spoken to Craig for long.

"You sound like you've really thought about this."

"I've spent the past four years studying for a PhD in astrophysics."

My jaw dropped, and my reflection in the window bore a remarkable resemblance to a goldfish. "A PhD? But I thought you were a model?"

"Just a pretty face, huh?" He sounded peeved. "The two aren't mutually exclusive, you know. Don't you get annoyed when men make that assumption about you?"

"I wouldn't know. Men never do."

"You're kidding?" He gave his head a little shake. "Whatever. Modelling pays better than science, so I plan to make as much cash as I can before my face falls out of favour and use it to fund my next research project."

Oh. This guy surprised me more with every passing minute. From the way he'd helped me clean his car rather than phoning the police, to his choice of career versus passion. I only wished I'd met him under different circumstances, although if I had, I'd probably have been too nervous to speak to him. Girls like me didn't mix with geniuses or pin-up boys, and Lachlan was both.

"That's, uh..."

"Mercenary?"

"Sensible. Better than living on student loans. Not that I'm suggesting you're in debt at the moment.

Although if you are, that's perfectly acceptable in this day and age, especially if you've been researching important things like...stars?" *Cherry, stop talking. You're clearly too stupid to be having this conversation.* "I'm going to be quiet now."

A *ping* sounded, and Lachlan fished his phone out of his pocket. Saved by the bell. Thank goodness. I took a sip of wine, a smooth Chardonnay with a hint of citrus, and leaned back against the counter as he scrolled through a message. His lip twitched as he read. A smile? Curiosity? Or merely concentration?

Finally, he looked up, but I couldn't read his expression.

"Three point five? That's harsh."

I choked on my mouthful of wine, and I was so busy coughing that the smash as the glass hit the floor barely registered. He knew? How the hell did he know?

"Shit, I'm sorry," he said. "Don't move or you'll cut your feet."

I'd slipped my shoes off in the hallway out of habit, and now Lachlan picked me up and set me on the counter before he fetched a dustpan and brush from under the sink.

"I'm sorry. I'm so sorry," I spluttered. "But how...?"

"A friend from university forwarded me the email." He grimaced. "I'm afraid it seems to be spreading."

I closed my eyes and thunked my head back against a cupboard door. "Which university?"

"Hertfordshire."

"That's not even in the same county."

"If it makes you feel better, some of the guys have added comments. You've scored four nines and five tens, and half a dozen of them reckon Craig's a prick."

"But they still sent the message on."

"Yeah, they did."

"Dammit. I need a proper drink." I twisted around and opened the cupboard where Craig used to keep the spirits, but all I found was two kinds of muesli and a packet of wholewheat spaghetti.

"Easy, easy." Lachlan rested a hand on my thigh as he reached past me and came back with a bottle of Gordon's Gin. "You want tonic with it? Or are you upset enough to drink it neat?"

"I guess I should have tonic unless I want to add 'alcoholic' to my list of shortcomings."

He took a fresh glass out of the dishwasher and poured me a generous measure, even adding a slice of lemon and a few ice cubes.

"Thanks."

I chugged half of it back and gave myself brain freeze. How far had that email got? I was almost naked, for goodness' sake, and that pink-and-red underwear was far from my best set. Maybe I could emigrate? Go and bake apple strudel in Austria or baklava in Turkey...

"You might want to go easy on that," Lachlan said, eyeing up my glass.

"No, I don't."

"It wasn't that bad."

"How? How was it not that bad?"

"He said you were okay in bed."

"Okay? Just okay? Mediocre. Average. Hardly glowing praise, was it?"

"And no man wants a woman who's easy. Worth the effort, yes. Easy, no."

"Craig did."

"Then I'd say you were pretty accurate with what you wrote on my bonnet. But as I mentioned earlier, your approach was wrong. Behaving like that would have only reinforced his opinion of you. The way to gouge him is by making him realise he made a huge mistake in letting you go."

I swallowed the rest of my drink and poured myself another. Lachlan didn't say anything, just passed me the ice-cube tray and a fresh slice of lemon.

"He's not missing anything, though, is he? That's the whole point. You've seen what he wrote about me— clingy, obsessed with tidying, and apparently I only like fancy restaurants. Just because I refused to go to the pub every time we went out..."

"I'm with you on the pub food."

"It's all fried. Everything. Even the bloody chicken." Boy, that gin tasted good. "I made him chicken—roast chicken, chicken fajitas, chicken cordon bleu, chicken stew, chicken Caesar salad, chicken paella... And still he preferred chicken nuggets with chips and beer while he watched football."

"Never saw the attraction of football myself."

I raised my glass and gin slopped over the sides. "Oops. But totally. Twenty men running around a field, kicking a bag of air, crying if they fall over."

"I believe there are eleven on each team."

"Huh?"

"So twenty-two men running around the field."

Did I detect a chuckle?

"Twenty, thirty, it doesn't matter. None of it matters anymore. Everyone in the south of England's probably seen that email by now, so I'm going to die alone."

The chuckle morphed into full-blown laughter. "He should have put melodramatic on the list."

"It's not funny."

"It kind of is. Look on the bright side—at least now the asshole's dentist is stuck making him six different kinds of chicken instead of you."

"I know I should feel relieved, especially now I've seen what he really thought of me, but I don't. I'm just..." I hid my face behind my hands. "Embarrassed."

"Well, you shouldn't be. Craig's the one who looks like an idiot. Keep your head, keep your dignity, and you'll get through this."

"It's a bit late for keeping my head after what I did to your car."

Lachlan sighed and took a sip from his own glass of wine. "Look, the car's clean, and I'm going to assume you suffered from a temporary breakdown. Let's forget it ever happened, okay?"

"A breakdown, yes. Thank you." I put a finger to my lips and giggled. "I'll forget I ever came here."

Apart from Lachlan's abs. I'd quite like to remember those from time to time. As a model, what were the chances of him having his own calendar? I could get a copy for my lounge. And another for the bakery and one for my bedroom. Would he sign them for me?

"Cherry? Are you okay?"

"Do you have a calendar?" I blurted.

"A what?"

"A calendar. You know, like with pic-shures of yooooou."

He reached out and gently peeled my fingers away from my glass. "I think you've had enough of this."

I may have been a teensy bit tipsy, but I realised how stupid I sounded. Lachlan's patience must have been wearing thin.

"You're right. Of course you're right. I'll call that cab." Only I'd left my phone in my handbag in the living room, and when I tried to go and get it, my feet didn't work properly and I sprawled across the floor in front of the cooker. So much for keeping my dignity.

"Shit," Lachlan muttered, hauling me upright. "Look, you sit on the sofa, and I'll sort out a cab."

"It's fine. I can do it, hornets...onits...honestly."

Whoops. Where did that table come from?

Lachlan scooped me up and deposited me in the lounge, where my head refused to stay upright on my shoulders as it lolled against the cushions. Wow. This sofa was so much comfier than Craig's. And Lachlan's bottom was so much firmer. My eyes began to close, but my ringing phone made them snap open again.

"Where ish it?"

Lachlan shook his head as he fished it out of my handbag and put it to his ear. "Don't try to move."

I made a brief attempt to get up, but my limbs were moving in funny directions. Perhaps he was right and I should have a little rest.

"Olivia?" I heard him ask.

What did she want? Ah yes, the axe murderer thing. "I'm fine," I tried to call out, but my voice was a croak. "No axe murderers."

Lachlan rolled his eyes. "I think you should come and get your friend. She's drunk half a bottle of gin, and she's about to pass out on the sofa."

I was? Really? I mean, I felt kind of sleepy, but...

CHAPTER 5

"SO YOU DRANK a little too much," Olivia said on Tuesday morning. "It happens to us all. I tripped over at a party last month after one too many cocktails."

I knew she was only trying to make me feel better, but it wasn't helping.

"But I was in the man's house. I must have drunk half of his alcohol stash before I ended up unconscious on his sofa."

"At least you didn't puke until you were halfway home."

Yes, that happened too. Olivia had to stop her car by the side of the road so I could throw up in a bush. Last Saturday went down in history as the single worst day of my life, beating even the time I'd gone skiing with Craig and broken my arm on the nursery slope. The hottest guy I'd ever met or was ever likely to meet, and I'd behaved so utterly, utterly badly that all I wanted to do was crawl into a volcano and burn in a hail of sparks. Although with my luck, I'd probably fizzle out like a damp squib.

"Lachlan must think I'm crazy."

"Lachlan? That's his name? Isn't that Scottish? He didn't sound Scottish."

"We didn't exactly discuss his heritage. I was too busy having a meltdown. He's probably composing a furious email to all his friends about the hysterical woman who decorated his car then went full alcoholic in his kitchen."

And that wasn't even the worst part. I liked him. I really liked him, and I'd made his life hell for an evening. He'd wanted a quiet Saturday night relaxing at home, and instead he'd ended up hosing syrup off his previously immaculate BMW and dealing with my inability to get dumped gracefully.

"He didn't seem angry, more amused," Olivia said.

Was it better or worse to have him laughing at me? "I'm never showing my face in Great Haseley again. From now on, I'm going to buy my groceries in the village and do the rest of my shopping online."

"I thought Lachlan said he wouldn't tell anybody about the car?"

"He did, but Craig promised he'd treat me with respect and look what happened."

I pounded the pastry I was making into the marble counter then grabbed a rolling pin. Baking usually made me happy, but even icing the cupcakes couldn't shift the black cloud hovering over me this week.

"Lachlan's not Craig," Olivia said. "I only spoke to him for a few minutes, but he seemed like a genuinely nice guy."

Yes. Yes, he was.

"I think I need a cake. For medicinal purposes, you understand."

Olivia grinned and headed for the centre island, where she'd just transferred a batch of strawberry cheesecake muffins onto a cooling rack.

"Dr. Olivia prescribes a cup of tea, a muffin, and a cookie if you're still feeling miserable."

One cookie? I needed at least a dozen.

By Saturday, I'd put on three pounds and worked twelve hours of overtime to keep myself busy. Every time I paused, Lachlan popped back into my mind, looking at me with disapproval. Last night, I'd dreamed of him too. Okay, so it was more of a nightmare—we'd started off in his kitchen, and every time I took a not-so-delicate sip of gin, I'd floated further away, until I found myself marooned on a distant planet with only Craig and his dentist for company.

"Thanks for all your help this week," Olivia said. "I couldn't have got everything done without you, and Milicent Morton's daughter was thrilled with the roses you made for her mother's eightieth-birthday cake."

"Sugarcraft was always my favourite subject at catering college."

"It shows." Olivia checked everything was turned off in the kitchen before picking up her handbag. "Are you sure you don't want to come out with us tonight?"

Olivia and a few of her girlfriends were heading to an Italian restaurant in Great Haseley, and although she'd promised a table in a quiet corner and plenty of alcohol-free cocktails, I couldn't bring myself to go out in public yet. An evening of Netflix beckoned, and maybe tomorrow I'd get around to painting my kitchen. In line with my new shopping policy, I'd ordered two tins of Lemon Ice matt emulsion from the internet, plus the brushes and drop cloths to go with them. A pale yellow kitchen would be so much more pleasant than Agnes's avocado walls, but a big part of me wanted to spend two days curled up with cake and tissues instead.

As if reading my mind, Olivia waved a hand in the direction of the shop. "Help yourself to whatever you want to eat. We'll need to make fresh pastries on Tuesday, anyway."

Jogging shoes. I should order jogging shoes as well, and maybe a tracksuit.

"Thanks, and have a lovely dinner."

Once Olivia had gone, I surveyed the contents of the display case. Individual fruit flans, maple-pecan cupcakes, pineapple-and-banana muffins—those were a favourite among the socialites because they gave the illusion of being healthy. Millefeuille, croissants, a couple of mini apple pies. Far too much for me to eat, and apart from the fruit cakes and the protein flapjacks, which would keep for weeks, we'd be throwing it all away on Tuesday morning.

Hmm... Maybe I should take a small selection around to Lachlan to apologise? No need to speak to him—I could just leave the box on the doorstep with a note and run.

Before I could rethink the idea, I packed half a dozen sweet treats into a box and gift-wrapped it with lots of ribbons and a bow, making sure to include the low-fat and fruit varieties after his comment about watching his figure. Then I took them all out and put them into another box that didn't look quite so girly.

"Am I really going to do this?" I muttered to myself.

The alternative meant eating all the pastries myself while feeling like a cow because I hadn't told him how sorry I was. No, this was a good idea. In fact, I should have done it earlier. I considered refreshing my hair and make-up, but after Craig knocked points off for that, I thought the better of it and settled for running a comb through and adding a touch of lip gloss.

I'd barely driven my little old Toyota since I moved to Northbury, but the engine coughed into life on the second attempt, and I set off. Three times I nearly turned back, even circling a roundabout for ages before I carried on towards my old home. At the final set of traffic lights, I tapped my fingers on the steering wheel as I waited for the green. The last time I'd travelled this route, I'd been fuelled by anger rather than guilt, and it had been a whole lot easier.

Maybe Lachlan wasn't in? After all, it was Saturday night, and he surely had better things to do than sit at home with cakes and box sets. He was probably out in town, having—

Oh, there was his BMW, parked up in the driveway.

The smart thing to do would have been to leave the box inside the porch, back out of the drive, and be home in time for *Strictly Come Dancing*, but I was Cherry Sanders and "stupid" was my middle name. My fingers rang the bell before I could stop them, and seconds later, footsteps sounded on the stairs.

The door opened.

"It's you."

Lachlan peered down at me, hair artfully mussed, and I thrust the box in his direction.

"Y-y-yes. I brought cakes. And an apology. Well, I didn't bring the apology, exactly, but I came to make it because I'm really sorry for the way I behaved last week."

He stepped outside and pulled the door closed, forcing me to back up a couple of steps. "You know, the more I think about that, the funnier it was. I bet I'm the only guy in the county to get his car turned into a birthday cake. Good thing you didn't get as far as adding the candles."

"But it wasn't just that. Afterwards..."

"At least you lay down rather than throwing up."

"No, I saved that for the trip home." I raised my eyes to the sky. "Dammit, I didn't mean to tell you— Hey, what's that? Is it a shooting star?"

Lachlan turned and followed my gaze, smiling. "The Perseid meteor shower. I've been watching them all evening from the back deck."

"The one off the master bedroom? I used to love sitting out there in the summer."

"That deck was the reason I rented this house. The place is bigger than I need and more than I wanted to pay, but once I stepped out there, I was sold. It's perfect for watching the show tonight, especially with the sky so clear."

"So, what exactly is a shooting star?"

"It's not a star at all. What you saw was a meteoroid, a tiny piece of rock that burned up as it entered the earth's atmosphere."

"Do you think there'll be more tonight?"

"At least fifty per hour."

"I wish I still had a garden so I could sit out and watch them."

That was one thing I missed while living in Agnes's flat—the lack of outside space. A few pansies in a window box just wasn't the same.

Lachlan paused then took a step back, opening the door. "Why don't you watch from the deck with me? As long as you don't have plans, that is."

"Really?"

He shrugged. "There's plenty of space. And thanks for the cakes."

CHAPTER 6

"DO YOU WANT a drink?" Lachlan asked.

"Something non-alcoholic?"

"That's probably for the best. Tea? Coffee? Juice? Hot chocolate?"

"You have hot chocolate?"

His cheeks coloured a little. "Guilty secret. My mum used to make it for me every evening when I was a kid."

"I'd love a cup."

He pushed the door wide enough for me to fit past him and followed me into the kitchen. I reached for the kettle automatically, then stopped myself.

"Sorry. Keep forgetting I don't live here anymore."

"Why don't you find a plate for the cakes? They're in the cupboard under the microwave."

Ten minutes later, we were sitting cross-legged up on the deck. Lachlan had laid out a thick blanket, and we leaned back against the house wall with the cakes and drinks between us as we looked up at the sky.

He motioned at the fancy-looking telescope beside us. "Let's eat these first, and then I'll show you how to use that. You'll be able to see a lot more with it."

"Hey, look! Another meteor." The white dot streaked across the sky right ahead. "They're so pretty." I took out my phone and snapped a photo. "Aw, it's all blurry."

Lachlan stepped into his bedroom and came back with a camera to rival the telescope. "Here, try this. I can email you the pictures."

"I don't even know how to turn it on."

He leaned over to show me, and each time his fingers brushed mine, a zing of electricity surged through my veins. My hands were shaking by the time I raised the viewfinder to my eye. Did he realise the effect he had on me? I took a few photos of the sky, then snuck a glance at the man next to me. His gaze was fixed on the stars, both hands clasped around his mug of hot chocolate.

"Did you always want to be an astronomer?"

"Astrophysicist, but I won't bore you with the differences. Yes, since I was little. My father bought me my first telescope for my seventh birthday. We lived in Northumberland, and the skies were so much darker up there, but he had to move down south to work when I was a teenager."

"I've never really looked at the sky, but it's so beautiful."

"Give your eyes half an hour to adjust to the dark, and it'll be even more spectacular."

"Do you know the names of all the stars?"

"Just the main ones." He pointed out a cluster of stars up ahead. "The Perseid meteor shower is named after the constellation Perseus because it radiates out from there."

"They've come all that way?"

"No, they just look like they have. They've actually come from the comet Swift-Tuttle. See that bright dot over there?"

I followed his finger. "Mmm."

"That's Alpha Persei, and Beta Persei is that one just across from it."

Another meteor lit up, and I grabbed the camera. "Got it!" Then another flash of light, and another. "Hang on, why is that one going in a different direction?"

"It's a late meteor from the Delta Aquarid shower that started in July. There'll be more of those in the early hours."

I finished the fruit flan and my hot chocolate while Lachlan ate the apple pie. This evening was crazy weird, but a good weird. Who knew stars could be so interesting?

"Are you ready to try the telescope?" he asked.

"Why not?"

Only before I could stand, my phone buzzed with a message from Olivia.

Olivia: Please don't freak out, but there's a new email going around. A comparison of you versus the dentist. She probably sent it herself, the nasty troll.

I gulped in a breath and scrolled down. Nothing. Where was the message?

Cherry: Do you have a copy?

Olivia: Not yet, I only heard about it a few minutes ago. Are you okay? Do you want me to come over?

"What's wrong?" Lachlan asked. "You're shaking."

I passed my phone over, and the faint light from the screen showed his eyes narrowing.

"If this is true, I'm half-tempted to go round and help you chuck shit over his car myself. Do you need a proper drink?"

"No!" I shook my head vehemently. Craig had ruined last weekend, and tonight I was enjoying myself for the first time since our split. I'd be damned if he was going to wreck that for me too. "Can we just look through the telescope?"

Lachlan sounded doubtful. "Are you sure?"

"I don't want to think about it, okay?"

"Okay." He got to his feet and offered me a hand. "One lesson in astronomy coming up."

Lachlan's smooth voice made my insides go full roller coaster as he guided me through the settings on the telescope, but what made me forget everything, even which planet I lived on, was the warmth of his arms as he reached around my body to help me find each star he spoke about. He must have spent an hour describing galaxies, constellations, and planets, but all I remembered was the way he pressed up against me. I think I managed to nod in the right places, and while I couldn't have told Mars from the Milky Way, what he showed me was beautiful.

"It's getting chilly," he said when he finally stepped back.

"It is?" I blew out a breath, and the air steamed a little even though it was August. But my insides were on fire. "Oh, yeah. It is."

"Must be the clear sky. Great for stargazing, not so good for staying warm. I'll grab my duvet."

"What for?"

"So we can lie down and watch the rest of the show." A hint of doubt crept into his voice. "Unless you don't want to?"

The chance to spend more time with Lachlan? Of course I wanted to. "I'd love to stay."

He dropped the pillows off his bed onto the blanket then pulled the duvet over us, and although he didn't touch me, my heart began beating in a wild tattoo. This evening had given me more of an insight into the man at my side—kind, clever, a closet geek overshadowed by a handsome face. I liked everything I'd found out about him, and when my phone buzzed again, I almost threw it over the railing.

"Aren't you going to check that?" he asked.

"I'm not sure I want to know."

"Is not knowing better?"

"No, you're right." What had my mother always told me? *Forewarned is forearmed.* Yes, it was another message from Olivia.

Olivia: Okay, I've tracked the email down. It's not good, I'm afraid. Just delete it if you don't want to see.

I clicked on the file, and another photo of me in my underwear popped up. Taken from the same set, this one showed me at an angle, with a slight stomach pooch and my mouth open, no doubt telling Craig to stop taking bloody photos. Next to me, the dentist beamed at the camera in a lace bra and matching panties that left nothing to the imagination, her massive boobs making her waist look even tinier.

And underneath?

3.5 vs 11/10

Hit the jackpot with my new girl!

- Can name every member of Arsenal's squad, including the reserves.

- Sucks like a vacuum cleaner.

- Free dental care.

- Never has to queue at the bar.

- Cooks an awesome fry-up on a Sunday morning.

How could I have been so stupid? Why didn't I see who Craig really was in the four years we were together? I mean, if I'd known sucking like a Hoover rather than using one to clean the house was all that was required, I could have saved myself hours of effort every week. It wasn't as if it took long to get Craig off—I could count the number of times I'd come first on one hand.

"Hey, don't cry." Lachlan raised his thumb to wipe my cheek.

"I'm sorry. It's just... You might as well see. I'm sure it'll turn up in your inbox eventually, anyway."

He was silent for a few seconds then let out a long breath. "Let's watch the stars. Forget that email for tonight. We'll deal with it in the morning."

We'll deal with it? Since when had there been a 'we'? But I wasn't about to argue if Lachlan wanted to lie here and watch nature's light show with me. Instead, I relaxed back against a pillow that smelled of him and waited for the next meteor to appear.

CHAPTER 7

WHERE WAS I? I took stock of the soft mattress underneath me and the duvet over the top, then cracked an eyelid open. The familiar sight of the patio doors leading out to the bedroom deck caused me to sigh. I was in Lachlan's bed, but he wasn't with me.

He must have put me here, but when? I'd awoken in the early hours snuggled into his side on the blanket next to the telescope, and he'd still been asleep then. Maybe I should have got up and gone home, but I'd been too content to move. Was he upset that I'd stayed the night? I mean, he hadn't invited me to, but he hadn't asked me to leave either.

I rolled out of bed and padded down the stairs, following the smell of bacon to the kitchen.

"Hi," I said.

Lachlan flipped a rasher of bacon with a spatula then smiled. "I hope you didn't have any important plans this morning. You looked like you needed the sleep, so I left you in bed."

"No, I've got the day off. What time is it?"

"Almost noon. Do you want bacon, or would you prefer something else?"

"Bacon's good. What happened to your diet?"

"I have a bacon roll every Sunday, and then it's back to the healthy stuff."

"Do you need a hand?"

"Can you get the baguette out of the oven?"

This felt too comfortable, sharing a kitchen with Lachlan like I'd never moved out. Except the kitchen had always been my domain, and mine alone. Craig had never cooked, only picked up takeout on occasion. I cut the baguette in half, put one piece on each of the plates Lachlan had left out, and carried them over to the stove.

"Does this feel odd to you?" I asked.

"Yeah."

That was it? Yeah? What did that even mean? I was none the wiser as Lachlan collected a bottle of ketchup from the fridge and set the bacon rolls out on the breakfast bar in front of his open laptop. A familiar figure looked back at me from the screen, although I wished I'd never laid eyes on her. The dentist, posing in front of a full-length mirror in a red evening dress. The bedroom behind her looked a tip.

Underneath, she'd written a note to her friends: *Got my dress for the Rubies and Roses charity do! The event to be seen at, and I'm gonna be the belle of the ball!*

Forty-seven likes and twenty-two comments telling her how fabulous she looked, mostly from men. I was just amazed her cleavage hadn't fallen out.

"Why are you looking at Shelley's Facebook page?"

"Remember what I said about revenge? The way to hit Craig where it hurts is to make him regret ever giving you up."

"How?"

Lachlan took a bite of his breakfast and flipped to the next browser tab. "By going to that ball, looking stunning, and acting classy."

Bloody hell, he'd bought two tickets. "Are you kidding?"

"I may be a geek, but I promise you I scrub up well."

"You're coming with me? Like a date?"

He shrugged and looked a little sheepish. "I was kind of hoping to."

"But why, after everything I've done?"

"Because I like that you're tidy and enjoy fancy food, and that you don't jump into bed with every man you meet and you dress up to go out. The jury's still out on the sparkles, but I rate you a hell of a lot higher than three point five." He grinned, and my knees went wobbly. "So, what do you say?"

"I've never been to a ball before."

"All you have to do is eat the food and smile."

"What about dancing? I don't know how to dance."

"It's not mandatory."

His smile faltered, and for the first time I realised he might be nervous too.

"Okay, I'll come."

He reached out to squeeze my hand. "It's a date, then."

When I got home, Olivia was pacing downstairs in the bakery with two bottles of wine on the counter next to her.

"Where have you been? You haven't been answering your phone. I was about to call the police."

I fished it out of my bag and realised I'd knocked

the button onto silent by mistake. Whoops. "I'm so sorry. I didn't hear it ring."

"I got worried in case you'd done something silly. Maybe I shouldn't have told you about that message, but I thought you had a right to know."

"It doesn't matter anymore. Just because Craig thinks of me that way doesn't mean every other man will."

"You've changed your tune since yesterday. Not that I'm complaining, of course, because I totally agree with you, but what happened to dying alone with nobody to mourn your passing?"

"Uh..."

Olivia put her hands on her hips. "Cherry, I'm your friend. Don't keep secrets from me."

"Okay, okay. I went to see Lachlan."

"Lachlan whose car we modified last week?"

"I went to apologise properly, and he's not mad about that anymore."

"Why are you smiling like that?"

"Like what?"

"Oh my gosh! You've been there all night. Did you do it with the sexy science guy?"

"No! We talked for ages then fell asleep on the back deck watching a meteor shower."

"That's so romantic. At least, I think so. Meteors?"

"It was friendly. Comfortable."

"But you like him?"

"Yes, I do. And this morning he came up with a plan for revenge, mark two."

"I like him more and more. Look, I brought wine in case you needed it, but it's kind of early for that. Why don't we head up to your flat for tea and cakes, and you can tell me all the good bits?"

There wasn't that much to tell, but a cup of tea sounded like a good idea. My mouth had gone dry just thinking about my date next Saturday night, not to mention how I was going to lose the three pounds I put on last week before then. And a dress, I needed a dress. Not a tarty red number like Shelley's, but a proper ball gown.

"Where can I get a posh dress around here? Is there a hire shop?"

"What for?"

"Because Lachlan's taking me to the Rubies and Roses charity ball next weekend."

Olivia turned halfway up the stairs and grinned. "Ooh, I'm going to that one too with Nye. Don't worry; I can sort dresses for us. Do you want to sit at our table? I know the organiser, and I'm sure she won't mind shuffling things around a bit."

A few more friendly faces? Maybe I could survive the evening after all. "If it's not too much trouble."

"No trouble at all. But tell me, how does this fit in with revenge plan B?"

Twenty minutes later, I'd explained everything to Olivia, and she clapped her hands together in glee.

"I hate to admit it, but that might be even better than the corn syrup and marshmallows. Why don't you come round tomorrow and you can try on some of my dresses? Nye's grandma's always buying me new ones, and I haven't even worn half of them. We're about the same size."

I threw my arms around her. "I don't know what I'd do without you."

"Well, you wouldn't have ended up washing a hot

guy's car, that's for sure."

Monday afternoon found me knocking on the door of the east wing at Northbury Hall, the magnificent manor house Olivia called home. She shared the wing with her fiancé, Nye, while Nye's parents occupied the west wing and his grandma lived in an annexe to the rear. Ivy made me a little nervous, but Olivia assured me she had a heart of gold.

"Ivy's a darling, honestly," she'd said on more than one occasion. "It's Nye's mother who scares me. She still doesn't think I'm good enough for her son."

And it was Ivy and Olivia who were waiting for me today. Barely noon, and Ivy handed me a champagne flute as I walked through the door.

"Don't worry, I'll ask my chauffeur to drop you home. You can pick up your car tomorrow."

Her opening words were a good indication of how the afternoon was to go. By five, we'd got through a bottle of Veuve Clicquot between us, we'd tried on half the outfits in Olivia's dressing room, and Ivy was snoring away on the sofa.

"Is she okay?" I whispered.

Olivia glanced across. "Oh yes. She often has a nap around this time. It means she can keep going all evening. When I'm her age, I only hope I've got her stamina."

I made one final turn in front of the mirror. "You think this is the right dress?"

The floor-length green silk number hugged my curves in all the right places, and although I couldn't compete with the dentist's implants, my cleavage at least looked half-decent above the cowl neck. Lacy cap sleeves offset the thigh split and made the dress look elegant rather than risqué.

"Definitely. Ivy's booked the hairdresser for after work, and he's going to do something with rosebuds. Ivy's also promised to lend us some of her rubies. Believe me, she's got plenty."

Ivy was coming to the ball too, in a dark pink satin dress that only one in a hundred ladies her age could pull off. Her date for the evening would be her friend Marlene, who was on her way from America to visit.

"I'm still worried about this."

"Which part? Going with Lachlan or Craig being there?"

"Both."

"Lachlan wouldn't have suggested the idea if he wasn't keen on you, and I've already spoken to the organiser. We'll all be on a table at the front, and she's relegated Craig and Shelley to the back near the toilets."

A smile crept onto my face. "I don't suppose Shelley'll like that."

"No, I don't suppose she will."

Chapter 8

LACHLAN OFFERED TO pick me up for the ball in his BMW, but Ivy insisted on booking town cars for everybody.

"Far easier to go with it," Olivia whispered when I tried to decline. "She always wins these arguments."

After work, I hitched a lift to Northbury Hall with Olivia, and we got ready together. The stylist turned our hairdos into works of art, all elegant twists and curls with roses woven through them. My make-up took half an hour, but I avoided going for a heavy look —bronze eyeliner rather than black, pale pink lips, and a hint of blusher. The necklace Ivy lent me sparkled under the lights, and I was glad Nye worked for some sort of security company because I'd have been scared to wear it out alone. He'd never been anything but pleasant to me, but he exuded a dangerous aura that Olivia didn't seem to notice.

The driver picked Nye, Olivia, and me up from Northbury Hall first, then drove on to Great Haseley to fetch Lachlan. He was waiting at the door for us, and my heart skipped when he slid in beside me wearing a tuxedo that must have been custom made. Smooth jaw, slicked-back hair, a hint of aftershave—he did indeed scrub up well, and at that moment it was clear why he'd decided to concentrate on modelling for now.

"You look beautiful," he whispered, brushing my ear with his lips.

"So do you. Handsome. I mean, you look handsome." Darn it—I couldn't think straight around him.

He chuckled and squeezed my hand. "No need to be nervous. Just be yourself, and Craig'll get the message."

How could I explain that I'd forgotten Craig the moment I saw Lachlan this evening? I was more scared of messing things up with the man I'd spent every spare minute thinking about for the last week than worrying about an idiot who'd hurt me three times in the last two months.

The answer was, I couldn't explain it, so I smiled and nodded instead. Nye fiddled with his phone while Olivia made small talk, asking Lachlan about his studies and what he thought of living in Great Haseley. I barely took any of it in.

And then we arrived outside the upmarket hotel where the ball was being held. Pink lights shone on Kendall Grange in honour of this evening's charity, a locally based group raising money for breast cancer research. A pink carpet led from the steps at the front into the hotel, and a photographer waited to take our pictures as the chauffeur stepped out to open our door.

"Don't forget to smile," Lachlan whispered as he linked his arm through mine.

Easier said than done. I glanced around for any sign of Craig as I concentrated on not tripping over the edge of the carpet. I'd borrowed Olivia's shoes too, and the heels were higher than any of mine.

"Lachlan Manning?" the photographer asked.

He nodded his confirmation.

"How does it feel to be the new face of Ishmael's fashion line in the UK?"

He was what? I may not have been totally up to date with the current trends, but even I'd heard of Ishmael. Last week, *Vogue* magazine had called him the new Alexander McQueen, and he'd once dressed a movie starlet in a dress made entirely from orange peel.

"Working with him promises to be an interesting experience."

"When's your first shoot?"

"Couple of weeks."

"Would you mind posing for a few pictures?"

"No problem."

"Who's your date?"

Lachlan didn't let go of me, and the photographer grinned as he snapped away.

"This is Cheryl Sanders."

"Hang on. Isn't that the girl from that email? Miss three point five?"

"If you want any more photos of me, you won't mention that bullshit again."

The guy gulped. "Yeah, sure. Never saw it. She looks more like a ten to me, anyway."

"She most definitely is."

As soon as we got through the front door, I began apologising again. "I'm sorry. If I thought this would impact on your career—"

He silenced me by pressing his lips against mine, the first time he'd kissed me. Sparks shot through my veins all the way to my toes, even though it only lasted a second.

"It won't make the slightest bit of difference to my career. And stop saying you're sorry. I'm not, because if the idiot hadn't sent that email, I'd never have met you."

"Speaking of the idiot," Nye muttered, inclining his head to the left.

Craig stopped, slack-jawed, as Lachlan fixed him with a glare and I mustered up a smile. Not for Craig, but for the situation. My ex didn't look happy at all.

"Babe, what's up?" the dentist asked, following his gaze. "What's *she* doing here?"

Lachlan answered for both of us, voice sweet as honey. "Attending the ball, just like everybody else."

The dentist stepped forward, teetering on five-inch heels. She seemed to have missed the "ball" memo, because her dress stopped at mid-thigh.

"No way are you dating Lachlan Manning."

In all honesty, I had no idea what I was doing with him, but I did get a small measure of satisfaction that she'd recognised his face.

Lachlan slid an arm around my waist, his fingers landing on my hip and searing me through the thin layer of silk.

"Why is that such a surprise?" he asked.

"Because...because...because she's so *plain*."

Shelley made it sound like a disease.

Lachlan opened his mouth to reply, but then a stranger in a suit walked past, looking me up and down.

"Nothing plain about you, love." He nodded at Shelley. "You must need your eyes tested."

I could have kissed the man, but a lady in a pale grey sheath dress rushed past to hug Olivia. "I'm so glad you made it. I've saved your party the best table, right next to the stage. Ooh, Lachlan Manning—I saw an L Manning on the guest list, but I didn't realise it was you."

"Always happy to support local charities."

"Wonderful, wonderful. Anyway, let me walk you through."

Shelley looked like she was sucking on a whole variety of citrus fruit as we passed her. Nye was close enough behind for me to hear his words.

"Careful, sweetheart. If you clench that jaw any harder, you'll crack a veneer."

My smile grew a little wider.

Marlene turned out to be from the same mould as Ivy, except with a different accent and a dress covered in sequinned roses. Our table of eight was rounded out by Nye's colleague Zander and a statuesque blonde who looked like the kind of girl Lachlan should be dating. But Lachlan barely glanced at her all night.

"Your kind of food?" he asked when the starters came out.

"Very much so."

The red pepper mousse tasted delicious, but when I risked a glance to the back of the room, I was happy to see Craig pushing his around the plate.

"Wine?"

"Just one glass, no more."

Conversation flowed, and not about football, rugby, or any other ball-related sport, apart from a brief mention of the Super Bowl by Marlene, who it seemed was a fan. The main course of chicken in white wine sauce was another hit with our table, and for once, I felt as though I fitted in. Funny how the darkest points in life could turn into the brightest, wasn't it?

Marlene and Ivy won a vineyard tour in the charity

auction, and the evening raised over fifty thousand pounds for charity. We knew this because the organiser asked Lachlan to step up and present the oversized cheque, so no matter how many times Shelley accidentally-on-purpose walked in front of the photographer, we all knew which picture would make the local paper next week.

"She was clenching her teeth again," he joyfully told me when he sat down.

Every so often, loud laughter drifted over from the table at the back, and I suspected Shelley wasn't sticking to the same one-glass policy as me. But while I'd needed alcohol to get through an evening out with Craig, I didn't miss it at all with Lachlan. I even managed to dance without tripping over his feet or mine.

"It's gone well, don't you think?" Olivia said on our way to the powder room at the end of the night.

"I couldn't have hoped for more."

"Are you going home with your hottie tonight?"

Was I? I'd carefully been avoiding that question all evening. "I don't know. He hasn't even kissed me properly."

"Ah, but he wants to. That much is obvious."

"You think?"

"Cherry, he hasn't taken his eyes off you once tonight."

I pushed the door open, and Olivia squeezed past me, heading for the end stall.

"The only downside of my evening is this dress," she grumbled. "I had to wear two pairs of Spanx with it and going to the loo is a nightmare. I can't wait to get home and change into my nightie."

I giggled as I took the stall next to hers. "I'm sure Nye wouldn't have noticed if you hadn't worn the Spanx."

"Nye wouldn't have noticed if I'd worn a kaftan, but all the other women here would."

We both started laughing, which was perhaps why I missed the sound of the door opening. If I'd known Shelley was outside, I'd have hidden in the cubicle for the rest of the night.

But as it was, I almost walked into her on my way to the sinks, and she followed me, barbs flying.

"You bitch! How dare you turn up here and ruin my night?"

"I'm sorry?"

"This was my first big event with Craig, and you just couldn't stay away, could you? What did you do, rent Lachlan Manning by the hour just to show me up?"

Oh, she was beautifully angry, and slurring a little if I wasn't mistaken. "I'm not sure why you're so upset. Surely being seen next to a three point five would only make you look better? And you were the one who wanted Craig so much you stole him from me."

Material flapped behind me as Olivia battled her Spanx and flung the door open. "Don't be so bitter. Cherry's here to enjoy an evening with friends and raise money for charity, not to flaunt her bits in the hope of making the society pages like some people."

"How dare you..."

Olivia bent to wash her hands. "Not saying anything that isn't true."

"There's nothing wrong with wanting people to remember me."

"Whatever."

This time, Olivia held the door for me, and I scooted past, leaving Shelley and her nasty words behind us. Even then, she carried on.

"That's it, just walk away. You two are just a pair of plain Janes in expensive frocks. You wouldn't—"

Her words gave way to the sound of ripping fabric, and we turned back in time to see Shelley's flimsy dress get caught in the door and rip clean down the middle.

"Oh my goodness," Olivia whispered. "She's duct-taped her boobs together."

We weren't the only ones staring. The music from the string quartet in the corner came to a screeching halt as every person in the room stared in Shelley's direction. Apart from Craig. Craig sat down at the table and put his head in his hands.

I shouldn't have smiled, but I just couldn't help myself.

"Well, she got her wish. Everyone's going to remember her now."

CHAPTER 9

"THAT EVENING WENT better than I ever imagined," Lachlan said as he slipped an arm around my shoulders in the car.

Olivia began giggling again, and even Nye cracked a smile.

I burrowed in my clutch purse for another tissue. "Except my mascara's all smudged." Laughing until I cried had that effect.

"Mine too," Olivia said. "But it was worth it, especially after Shelley's bitchiness in the toilets. Karma kicked her in the backside."

"Your ex didn't look too amused either," Nye added. "Plus he kept staring at your ass in that dress."

Lachlan narrowed his eyes. "I didn't notice that part."

"Aw, don't get upset. I don't care how he looks at me anymore."

Because there was only one man I wanted now, the only trouble being I didn't quite know how to proceed with things. Lachlan hadn't mentioned going out again, and although I longed to ask, what if he said no? But he did have his arm around me. That had to count for something, right? I leaned closer into him, and one hand might have strayed to his thigh. His muscles stretched taut under my fingers, and I began to regret that little line in my unauthorised biography that suggested it took an effort to get me into bed. One snap of Lachlan's fingers, and I'd have dived onto the mattress.

The car stopped at Northbury Hall first to let Nye and Olivia out.

"I'll see you on Tuesday morning," she said, giving me a hug. "Enjoy the rest of the night."

One quick wink and they were gone, leaving me alone with Lachlan, nerves, and a large helping of indecision.

"Shall I drop you off next, Miss Sanders?" the driver asked.

"Yes, please."

The closer we got to the bakery, the more I wished we were heading for Great Haseley. I wasn't ready for this night to end. Should I say something? I stared out the window, hoping for divine inspiration, and by some miracle, I got it.

"Hey, look—a meteor."

"Where?" Lachlan leaned over to get a better view. "That's a good one."

"Is it another Perseid?"

"They'll be going for a few more days, although not so frequently as last weekend."

"Can we watch them again tonight?" The words slipped out before I thought about them. "Unless it's too late. Or too cold. Or you're busy."

He turned my chin so our eyes met. "You want to stay at my house tonight?"

The surprise in his voice mirrored my own shock that I'd even suggested it. "Uh, it was just a thought."

"You can stay any night you want, Cherry. Do you

need to pick up some clothes? Much as I like that dress, I doubt it's comfortable to sleep in."

"Maybe I could run in and grab a few things?"

The driver pulled up outside the bakery, and my fingers were shaking so much I could barely get the key in the lock. Then it took me two goes to input the alarm code, and we nearly ended up with our second drama of the night. Thankfully, the company Nye worked for monitored the security system, so they'd have called him rather than the police.

Upstairs, I went into panic mode. A suitcase was too much—I didn't want to scare Lachlan off—leaving me the choice of my carry-on bag or a small rucksack. Which of them said "casual night at a friend's house"? And more importantly, what should I pack?

Because despite Lachlan's easy agreement to me staying, I didn't know his intentions, and turning up in a lacy negligee when he expected flannel pyjamas would be mortifying. I pulled out a nightie and threw it back into the wardrobe. Too grandma. Black silk pyjamas. Classy without being overtly sexy? They'd have to do, as I couldn't come up with a better plan. Okay, I also needed clothes for tomorrow, and toiletries, and I should brush my teeth... Darn it; I'd taken ten minutes already.

By the time I got back outside, Lachlan was staring through the window, chewing his lip, while the driver snoozed in the front.

"Sorry, sorry. Time ran away from me."

Lachlan opened the door, and I took my spot beside him.

"I was beginning to worry you'd changed your mind."

"What? No, of course not."

He tapped the driver on the shoulder, and the man woke with a start. "Sorry, sir. Not sure what happened there."

Oops.

The engine purred into life, and we glided back into the night. The nearer we got to Great Haseley, the faster my heart raced.

"Worried?" Lachlan asked.

"What makes you think that?"

"Your knuckles have gone white where you're gripping the edge of the seat."

So they had. I made a conscious effort to loosen my fingers and tried a smile. "Maybe a little worried."

"There's no need to be. You were fine last weekend, weren't you?"

"But that was different. Spur of the moment."

"We're not going to do anything you don't want to do."

I wanted to tell him I trusted him, that I did want to take things further, and even though in the past I might have hesitated, with him I felt differently. But what came out was, "I think I want to do you."

Lachlan's eyes widened as I clapped a hand over my mouth.

"That came out completely wrong."

"Did it?"

My cheeks heated. "No."

He started laughing. "Cherry, you're one special lady."

"Am I? You haven't even kissed me properly."

"A situation I intend to rectify as soon as I get you in private."

Suddenly, Great Haseley seemed a really long way away. "Can this car go any faster?"

Lachlan kept his word. The instant his front door clicked shut behind us, he dropped my bag and wrapped both arms around my waist.

"I've been wanting to do this since last week."

Rather than go straight for my lips, he trailed one finger along my jaw, leaving tingles in its wake, then bent to smell one of the roses in my hair.

"I don't know what Craig was thinking when he let you go, but his loss is my gain. Thank you for tonight. For the effort you made to look beautiful, for your company, and for coming back here with me."

"Thank you for not having me arrested when I trashed your car."

He chuckled, and then he kissed me.

The fire began where our lips touched. Then it travelled downwards, bursting into flames and incinerating the butterflies in my belly. His tongue teased mine, and I may have sighed as I leaned into him, gripping his arms as if he might disappear at any moment.

Only once I was well and truly breathless did he pull back.

"I didn't realise how hungry I was until I tasted you," he whispered.

I couldn't help myself—I pulled on the ends of his bow tie until it unravelled. When he didn't say anything, I started on his shirt buttons, revealing a smooth, toned chest and rippling abs. They twitched under my hands, warm to the touch.

He held me tighter, and his hardness pressed against my stomach, stoking the flames still higher as he gathered my dress in his elegant fingers.

"I love this dress. I'd love it more on my bedroom floor." He cupped my bottom with warm hands, my cheeks bare on each side of the thong I'd worn in anticipation of the main event.

"Then why are we still down here?"

He didn't hesitate, just picked me up and carried me upstairs, but rather than dropping me on the bed, he settled me gently onto my toes by the sliding window.

"Do you still want to watch the stars?"

"You mean...us, together...outside?"

His eyes sparkled as he nodded. "It's something I've always dreamed of doing."

The best part of the top deck was its seclusion. Mrs. Flanders to the right didn't have any windows facing in our direction, and the house to the left was hidden from view by a high leylandii hedge. As long as we didn't make too much noise, nobody would notice.

"We'll need that blanket again."

Before I could blink, Lachlan was hauling not one but three blankets outside to make the wooden deck comfortable, followed by his duvet and a couple of pillows.

"Better not rain," he muttered as he bent to collect a condom from his nightstand drawer.

"I'm not sure I'd stop, even for that."

He shrugged out of his jacket and shirt, then glanced downwards. "Care to do the honours?"

While he might have dreamed of sex under the

stars, my secret fantasy involved peeling a man out of his tuxedo and exploring every inch of him with my tongue. Craig hadn't even owned a suit.

Lachlan didn't disappoint. He wore a pair of well-fitted briefs under his trousers, and sprang free as I removed those too. The tongue thing would have to wait, because now he beckoned me upwards and reached around to undo my zip. Olivia's dress billowed to the floor, leaving me in my favourite set of underwear—pale pink silk edged with black lace. Nice, but a little naughty too.

One by one, the roses fell to the floor as Lachlan unpinned my hair, followed by my bra and panties. Only once we were both naked did he speak again.

"Ready to go outside, beautiful?"

My answer was to kiss him, and he lifted me over the threshold and settled me onto the blankets—thick and fleecy, perfect for a night under the sky. I went to lie down, but he shook his head.

"Stay kneeling. You're going on top. I want to look up and see you in front of the stars."

I'd never done that before, but with Lachlan, everything was possible. He'd opened up a new world for me, one that didn't revolve around football and the pub.

I waited for him to sheathe himself before lowering myself onto him, and then the magic happened. First an orgasm that blew my mind, and then as Lachlan spilled into me, a meteor streaked overhead, leaving a shining trail across the inky sky.

"Seems like the universe was impressed by that too," Lachlan murmured, smiling up at me.

I could barely speak, so I just brought his hand to

my mouth and kissed each knuckle as he brushed the fingers of his other hand down the curve of my hip.

"I discovered a new star tonight," he whispered, then smacked his own forehead with the heel of his hand. "I can't believe how cheesy that sounded."

"Cheesy works for me."

Lachlan could have read me rhymes from Hallmark greetings cards and I'd still have melted inside.

We tidied ourselves up, and Lachlan gripped my hand under the duvet as we both lay looking at Perseus and the worlds beyond. Two months ago, I'd sat in this same spot considering whether to take a flying jump off the balcony, but today, the only leap I wanted to make was into a future with Lachlan. He made science sexy and revenge sweet. Somehow, I'd survived the mess with Craig and come out on top in more ways than one.

A LITTLE EXTRA...

If you too would like the illusion of being healthy, here's the recipe for Olivia's pineapple and banana muffins. I love this recipe, and the best bit is you can make it with one bowl and no mixer—saves washing up!

PINEAPPLE AND BANANA MUFFINS

Ingredients

    225g wholemeal self-raising flour
    180g soft light brown sugar
    1 tsp ground cinnamon
    1/2 tsp bicarbonate of soda
    2 ripe bananas (medium sized)
    425g tin of pineapple chunks
    6 tbsp sunflower oil
    2 large eggs

What to do with it all

1. Drain the tin of pineapple and chop it into chunks.

2. Mash the bananas with a fork.

3. Mix the flour, cinnamon, bicarbonate of soda, and sugar in a bowl.

4. Add the oil, eggs, banana, and pineapple to the dry ingredients and stir it all together.

5. Divide the mixture into twelve muffin cups.

6. Bake at 160C / 350F / Glass Mark 4 until a cocktail stick comes out clean.

7. Enjoy!

Total prep time: 20 mins

Total number of utensils to wash up: 6

Total calories: I don't want to think about it.

WHAT'S NEXT?

The Blackwood UK series continues in Roses are Dead...

Roses are dead, Lily is blue,
The killer's escaped without leaving a clue.
Will he come back with flowers and more?
To end what he only started before...

Find out more here: www.elise-noble.com/roses

If you want to see more of Nye, he also appears in *Pitch Black*, the first book in my Blackwood Security series.

Even a Diamond can be shattered...

After the owner of a security company is murdered, his sharp-edged wife goes on the run. Forced to abandon everything she holds dear - her home, her friends, her job in special ops - she builds a new life for herself in England. As Ashlyn Hale, she meets Luke, a handsome local who makes her realise just how lonely she is.

Yet, even in the sleepy village of Lower Foxford, the dark side of life dogs Diamond's trail when the unthinkable strikes. Forced out of hiding, she races against time to save those she cares about. But is it too little, too late?

****WARNING****
If you want sweetness and light and all things bright,
Diamond's not the girl for you.
She's got sass, she's got snark, and she's moody and dark,
As she does what a girl's got to do.

Find out more here: www.elise-noble.com/pitch-black

If you enjoyed Cherry on Top, please consider leaving a review.

For an author, every review is incredibly important. Not only do they make us feel warm and fuzzy inside, readers consider them when making their decision whether or not to buy a book. Even a line saying you enjoyed the book or what your favourite part was helps a lot.

Want to stalk me?

For updates on my new releases, giveaways, and other random stuff, you can sign up for my newsletter on my website:
www.elise-noble.com

Facebook:
www.facebook.com/EliseNobleAuthor

Twitter: @EliseANoble

Instagram: @elise_noble

I also have a group on Facebook for my fans to hang out. They love the characters from my books almost as much as I do, and they're the first to find out about my new stories as well as throwing in their own ideas that sometimes make it into print!

And if you'd like to read my books for FREE, you can also find details of how to join my review team.

Would you like to join Team Blackwood?

www.elise-noble.com/team-blackwood

The Trouble Series
Trouble in Paradise
Nothing but Trouble
24 Hours of Trouble

Standalone
Life
A Very Happy Christmas (novella)
Twisted (short stories)

www.ingramcontent.com/pod-product-compliance
Lightning Source LLC
Chambersburg PA
CBHW020642130626
46552CB00003B/1359